Let fear disappear,

is here!

Join the Squad as they venture
into Lord Klukk's lair. Can they
discover the secret of the evil
villain's ghastly gas?

It's time to fight crime with slime!

Collect all the cool cards and check out
the special website for more slimy stuff:

www.slimesquad.co.uk

Don't miss the rest of the series:

THE SLIME SQUAD VS THE FEARSOME FISTS
THE SLIME SQUAD VS THE TOXIC TEETH
THE SLIME SQUAD VS THE CYBER-POOS
THE SLIME SQUAD VS THE SUPERNATURAL SQUID
THE SLIME SQUAD VS THE KILLER SOCKS

Also available by the same author,
these fantastic series:

COWS IN ACTION

ASTROSAURS

ASTROSAURS ACADEMY

www.stevecolebooks.co.uk

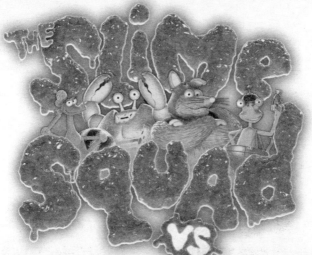

THE LAST-CHANCE CHICKEN

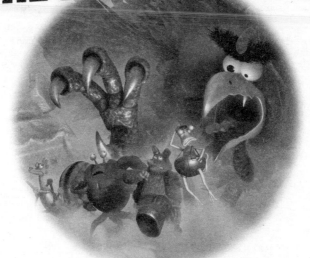

by Steve Cole

Illustrated by Woody Fox

RED FOX

THE SLIME SQUAD vs THE LAST-CHANCE CHICKEN
A RED FOX BOOK 978 1 862 30881 7

Published in Great Britain by Red Fox Books,
an imprint of Random House Children's Books
A Random House Group Company

This edition published 2011

1 3 5 7 9 10 8 6 4 2

The Random House Group Limited supports the Forest Stewardship
Council (FSC), the leading international forest certification
organization. All our titles that are printed on Greenpeace-approved
FSC-certified paper carry the FSC logo. Our paper procurement policy
can be found at www.rbooks.co.uk/environment.

Mixed Sources
Product group from well-managed
forests and other controlled sources
www.fsc.org Cert no. TT-COC-2139
© 1996 Forest Stewardship Council
FSC

Red Fox Books are published by Random House Children's Books,
61–63 Uxbridge Road, London W5 5SA

www.**kids**at**randomhouse**.co.uk
www.**rbooks**.co.uk

Addresses for companies within The Random House Group Limited can
be found at: www.randomhouse.co.uk/offices.htm

THE RANDOM HOUSE GROUP Limited Reg. No. 954009

A CIP catalogue record for this book is available from
the British Library.

Printed in the UK by CPI Bookmaque, Croydon

ONCE UPON A SLIME...

The old rubbish dump was far from anywhere. An enormous, mucky, rusty landscape of thousands of thrown-away things.

It had been closed for years. Abandoned. Forgotten.

And then Godfrey Gunk came along.

Godfrey wasn't just a mad scientist. He was a SUPER-BONKERS scientist! And he was very worried about the amount of pollution and rubbish in the world. His dream was to create marvellous mutant mini-monsters out of chemical goo – monsters who would clean up the planet by eating, drinking and generally devouring all types of trash.

So Godfrey bought the old rubbish dump as the perfect testing-ground and got to work.

Of course, he wanted to make good, friendly, peaceful monsters, so he was careful to keep the nastiest, most toxic chemicals separate from the rest. He worked for years and years . . .

And got nowhere.

In the end, penniless and miserable, Godfrey wrecked his lab, scattered his experiments all over the dump, and moved away, never to return.

But what Godfrey didn't know was that long ago, tons of radioactive sludge had been accidentally dumped here. And soon, its potent powers kick-started the monster chemistry the mad scientist had tried so hard to create!

Life began to form. Amazing mini-monsters sprang up with incredible speed.

Bold, inventive monsters, who made a wonderful, whiffy world for themselves from the rubbish around them – a world they named Trashland.

For many years, they lived and grew in peace. But then the radiation reached a lead-lined box in the darkest corner of the rubbish dump – the place where Godfrey had chucked the most toxic, dangerous gunk of all.

Slowly, very slowly, monsters began to grow here too.

Different monsters.

Evil monsters that now threaten the whole of Trashland.

Only one force for good stands against them. A small band of slightly sticky superheroes . . .

The Slime Squad!

Chapter One
SURPRISE!

Plog the monster stepped warily into the darkness of the massive cellar. Just one hour ago he had left his friends here while he popped out to the shops for some curdled flea-milk. Now, the lights had stopped working and the whole place seemed deserted.

"Hello!" Plog called, his long ears pricked for the slightest sound in reply, furry snout twitching for strange smells. Yes – he could smell something. Something sour and rotten and awful . . .

1

Tensing his tail and bunching his muscles ready for action, Plog crept forward. He was no ordinary monster – he was leader of the Slime Squad: the bravest, toughest, slimiest heroes in all Trashland. They had devoted their lives to defending their rubbish dump world from evil monsters that wanted to rule over it. And so if the base's power had shut down and all three of his fellow Squaddies – froggy Furp, crabby Danjo and skunky-poodle Zill – had suddenly gone missing, it might mean something bad had happened.

Something *very* bad.

Plog crept towards the office at the end of the passage, his orange fur wet with sweat. "PIE will know where the others are," he murmured.

The All-Seeing PIE was the Squad's super-computer boss – ever-alert to the slightest danger to innocent monsters, he watched over Trashland. Or at least, he *usually* did. But right now the office was thick with shadows and PIE's screen was dark.

"PIE?" Plog whispered fearfully. "You never normally switch off. What's happening around here?"

Suddenly he heard stealthy footsteps coming from the back of the office. "Hold it," he snarled, raising his fists. "Who's there?"

The lights switched on. Blinded for a moment, Plog gasped and dropped his flea-milk on the floor as a huge chorus went up: "SURPRISE!"

PIE's screen flicked on to show a huge smiley face – and there were Furp, Zill and Danjo standing at the back of the room. Danjo held a big cake in his powerful pincers. Zill held a large book in three of her six paws, and Furp was balancing a huge silver serving dish on top of his high-tech helmet.

"Thank goodness it's only you!" said Plog.

"Sorry to worry you," boomed PIE. "But our deception was necessary."

"Why?" Plog complained. "What's going on?"

Furp pointed to a large banner hanging down from the ceiling. It said: "HAPPY ANNIVERSARY!" Zill nodded.

"You've been leading the Slime Squad for six whole months, Fur-boy."

"Six months?" Plog blinked. "Then . . . that means it's also been six months since the first evil monsters turned up in Trashland."

"Correct – and it's only thanks to you that we stopped them," Furp said. "So we thought we'd hold a surprise party!"

"Right." With a dainty cough, Zill spat out a strand of slime at the ceiling, grabbed the sticky rope with her spare paws and swung across to join him. "To help celebrate, I've made you a special scrapbook of our adventures."

"And I baked you a cake," Danjo said proudly. "It's a dead-fly-and-fishbone sponge – your favourite!"

Overcome with emotion, Plog sniffed noisily – then wished he hadn't as the rotten smell invaded his nostrils again. "Urph! What's that weird whiff?"

"That is *my* contribution to the party," Furp announced, bouncing over with his silver platter. "Roast Cockroach *à la* Slime!"

He whipped away the silver cover – and the nuclear-strength niff nearly knocked Plog's nose off. "Urgh . . . I mean, er – what a lovely treat!" He looked at the massive squashed cockroach lying in a pool of pinky-yellow goo. "That looks—"

"Rubbish," said Danjo cheerily.

"Oh!" Furp looked hurt. "I know it smells a bit funny, but I'm sure it tastes delicious."

"And if it doesn't," said PIE, "you will find sick buckets in the storeroom."

"Now, let's get this party started," Zill declared. She spat out another slime-line, snagged the leg of a table laid for four and dragged it out into the centre of the room.

Danjo put down his cake, raised his left pincer and squirted steaming-hot slime into a bowl in the middle of the table.

"Put your platter down on top of that, Furp. If we have to eat your tum-curdling cockroach, at least we can have it warm!"

"Good idea." Furp placed his feast over the boiling bowl and hopped away.

"I'll fetch some fresh mould to sprinkle on top . . ." He climbed the wall using only his slimy palms and foot soles and started scraping black sludge from the ceiling into his metal pants. "Yum!"

But Plog barely noticed these preparations. His snout was stuck in Zill's scrapbook, which was stuffed full of newspooper clippings showing the Slime Squad in action. Plog saw himself fighting Fearsome Fists, tackling Toxic Teeth, scrapping with Cyber-Poos and Supernatural Squid and socking it to Killer Socks.

"All these monsters have one thing in common," Plog muttered.

Zill nodded. "Lord Klukk!"

"That evil mastermind is Trashland's public enemy number one," PIE declared. "And yet even with my all-seeing sensors, I know next to nothing about him."

"We've only ever seen him in shadow," Furp reflected. "Or spouting threats and bragging over a two-way smellyvision set."

"I wonder *why* he wants to take over Trashland," said Zill. "And why he's been so quiet lately. We haven't had any bad monsters to fight in weeks."

"Pity," said Danjo, eyeing the steaming cockroach with a grimace. "Fighting Klukk's pet monsters has got to be less dangerous than Furp's cooking!"

"Don't be rotten," said Zill.

"Why not?" Danjo chuckled. "The cockroach is!"

Furp looked a bit sad, so Plog took a deep breath, grabbed a big bit of cockroach and crunched it up.

It was revolting.

"Mmm," Plog said through a forced smile as he swallowed. "Delicious!"

Zill and Danjo ate a little too, holding their noses as they chewed.

Suddenly an alarm went off and PIE's screen flashed red and yellow. "Warning!" he boomed.

"I knew it," spluttered Danjo. "This stuff is poison, right?"

"Worse than that," said PIE. "My sensors are picking up something strange in the area of the Murky Badlands – the sinister squelch zone that borders Trashland's Darkest Corner . . ."

Zill swallowed hard – and not just because her mouth was full of slimy, smelly cockroach. "That's the lair of Lord Klukk!"

"Indeed it is," PIE agreed. "Look at this." His screen faded to show blank whiteness.

Danjo stared uneasily. "I don't see anything."

"Precisely," said PIE. "Right now this is the only thing you *can* see in the Badlands – thick white smoke, rolling out of the Darkest Corner like an ocean of fog."

"Extraordinary." Furp hopped closer to PIE's screen. "What is it?"

"Maybe Klukk's pumping out gas," said Plog. "*Poison* gas!"

Zill turned to PIE in alarm. "Is that possible?"

"My sensors can't tell in such a toxic area," PIE grumbled.

"Attention!" A loud, squawky and strangely muffled voice boomed out of the smoke on the screen. "Calling all slime-slinging fools! I am quite sure you are watching and listening *buk-buk*-by now . . ."

"That's Klukk's voice!" Zill whispered.

"Shortly I shall take over the whole of Trashland," the voice went on. "I expect you will want to try and stop me – so face me now! Come to the Murky *buk-buk*-Badlands if you dare . . . where I shall crush you once and for all!"

Chapter Two

MAGGOTS IN THE MIST

"I'm afraid your celebration must wait, Squaddies," said PIE. "You must drive out to the Badlands and investigate that sinister smog before it spreads too far into Trashland. We must learn what it is, what it does – and how to stop it!"

Plog stood up and stared around at his friends. "All of this started six months ago – it's time we ended it today."

Zill stood up too. "We'll make the anniversary celebrations into *victory* celebrations when we get back."

"*If* we get back," Furp said worriedly. "But don't worry." He pulled a plastic box from his circular pants and packed the leftover cockroach inside. "We can take dinner with us!"

"Great," said Plog as his tum gurgled. "Well, we'd better change into our costumes and split – we've got a mad, bad chicken-monster to smoke out!"

The sun was sinking as the Squaddies raced across Trashland in their supersonic invisible monster-truck, the Slime-mobile. Each of them was now dressed in their fighting outfits – a gold

leotard for Zill, glittering shorts for Danjo and Plog (though Plog wore his on his head as a kind of mask) and a golden crash-helmet-and-pants combo for Furp.

While Zill drove at top speed and Plog and Danjo waited tensely, Furp was busy in the lav-lab — his special space at the back of the Slime-mobile that was part laboratory, part toilet. Normally the toilet was used as a large, slimy mixing bowl for whatever incredible ingredients Furp was combining. But right now, Plog was so nervous he felt like using it in a different way . . .

Danjo eyed Furp curiously. "What are you up to?"

16

"Making gas masks for us all," Furp explained. "I don't know what that white smoke is, but I'm not in any hurry to breathe it in."

"Good thinking," said Plog.

"Meantime, we must finish off my Roast Cockroach *à la* Slime," Furp insisted, tossing over the box. "A good meal will set us up for the battle ahead."

Danjo groaned. "But what will a *bad* meal do?"

"Don't hurt his feelings," hissed Zill. "Thank you, Furp," she said more loudly, and politely nibbled a leg as she drove.

The journey continued in anxious silence. It was a long way to the Murky Badlands.

Furp plugged his crash helmet into one of the Slime-mobile's control panels to keep in contact with PIE.

"The white smoke is continuing to roll out from the Darkest Corner," the computer warned them. "At its current rate of advance it should reach the Mucky Mattress Marshes in a matter of hours."

Plog frowned. "The Marshes are full of mite-monsters. What will this white smoke do to them?"

"We must collect some for study," Furp called, hammering frantically at a white plastic faceplate. "There! That's my gas mask ready. I'll work on yours next, Plog."

Plog and Danjo chewed more gooey cockroach to pass the time. Furp finished it off as he completed Plog's mask and made a start on Zill and Danjo's.

Finally, after an hour or more, Zill braked sharply. "Look!"

Plog, Furp and Danjo gathered behind her and stared out through the windscreen. The Badlands were beige and bare, a muck-strewn wilderness. And in the distance, a huge wall of white smoke was blotting out the horizon, as though every kettle in Trashland had boiled all together. As tall as a cliff, the misty barrier whirled and seethed.

"I don't like the look of that," said Plog.

"I *must* have a sample for testing," said PIE over the Slime-mobile's screen.

Furp held up a dirty jar. "I'll go out and collect some."

"Sounds like a good time to test out this gasproof gizmo of yours," said Plog, picking up his gas mask.

"I wish you'd finished ours too," said Danjo. "I don't like to grumble – but I'm ready to rumble!"

"I'll finish them off as soon as I get back," Furp assured him.

Plog looked at Danjo and Zill. "Guys, if anything happens to us—"

"We'll drive in and rescue you," Zill said firmly. "Don't you worry."

"I won't." Plog smiled. "See you soon."

Putting their gas masks in place, Furp and Plog jumped down from the Slime-mobile and walked warily towards the swirling smoke, which was advancing like a rising tide. Plog was glad his feet were safely contained in heavy, water-filled, metal boots. If he ever took them off, his feet would leak outrageously stinky slime, so he imagined Furp was quite glad too – even if he *was* wearing a gas mask.

Suddenly Plog glimpsed movement deep inside the smog - a huge, dark shadow as big as a building. "Did you see that?"

"See what?" asked Furp. He checked his gas mask, pulled out his jar and unscrewed the lid. But as he neared the very edge of the whirling whiteness, a

21

deep, throaty chuckle sounded from within — and suddenly four burly maggoty monsters in glass helmets came racing out. Each held a large gun in their bony little hands — aimed at Plog and Furp.

"Maggot-men," Plog sneered. "Lord Klukk's pet hench-monsters. What's going on here? What's all the smoke?"

"Find out for yourself," said one of the maggot-men. "Pull off those masks and take a deep breath . . ."

"I recognize you." Plog glared at the maggoty monster. "Maynard, isn't it? You and your friend Marvin helped Lord Klukk with his plan to flood half of Trashland with the Supernatural Squid."

Maynard nodded. "You
his latest plan. Will they, Mar

The maggot-man beside him n
"Indeed they won't, Maynard. It just
can't fail."

"Unlike you, maggot-mush," Furp
cried – and suddenly hopped forward at
top speed, butting Marvin in the
stomach and knocking him into two of
his friends.

"Hold it, frog," snarled Maynard,
turning his gun on Furp.

"Hold *this*," Plog shouted, and kicked
out a foot so fast that his heavy boot
flew off and smashed into
Maynard's face – cracking
the glass helmet open
like a rotten egg.

g!" Furp brained
with his metal
hed Maynard's gun
ime, Plog's bare,
to drip toxic, super–

won't believe
...in?"
...dded.

"Ugh... ...rd screeched. Horrified,
he covered his nose and ran off in a
blind panic – too desperate to escape
the pong to realize he was heading
straight for the curling, whirling curtain
of white smoke . . .

"Come back here," Plog roared, starting after him.

"No, Plog!" Furp warned him. "We don't know what that smoke can do—"

But it was too late. Determined to catch the maggot-monster, Plog had already charged into the eerie, overwhelming gas cloud and vanished from sight . . .

Chapter Three
DEADLY CHICKEN

"Stop running away, Maynard!" Plog yelled as he pushed his way into the swirls of smoke. "You chicken!" But within seconds of entering this world of whiteness, he had to stop. Maggoty Maynard was nowhere to be seen.

I'm lost, Plog thought. Which way had he come from? Which way led to safety? Where had Maynard gone?

Suddenly something clucked in his ear. Plog jumped, gasped, raised his fists – and found Maynard right beside him, flapping his arms, stooped over and bobbing his head as if pecking at the ground.

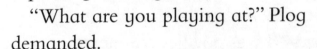

"What are you playing at?" Plog demanded.

But it seemed Maynard could not hear him. "Cluck!" he said simply. "Cluck, cluck!"

"You've been hanging around with your hen-faced boss too long. Come on, snap out of it. What's wrong with you?"

Plog looked at Maynard pecking the dirty ground. With his gas mask smashed, Maynard had been breathing the white smoke all this time. *Could the smoke have done something to him?* Plog wondered. *Perhaps it's made him go funny.*

"HA . . . HA . . . HA . . ."

Plog stared around wildly as a booming laugh cracked out above him with the force of a thunderclap. A shiver ran from his top to his tail bone. And suddenly he glimpsed something ahead – something thick and yellow and twisted like a giant tree trunk. Then it launched towards Plog and Maynard like a gigantic missile. There was no time to dodge aside. THWAM! The gnarled, yellowy thing smashed into the monsters

in its path and sent them flying through
the air.

"Whoaaa!"
Waving his arms,
Plog whooshed
straight out of the
fog, over Furp's
head and
crunched down on
top of Marvin and
the other two maggot-

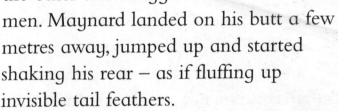

men. Maynard landed on his butt a few
metres away, jumped up and started
shaking his rear — as if fluffing up
invisible tail feathers.

"Plog!" Furp bounced up to join him.
"Are you all right? You flew out of that
smoke like a seagull with a bomb up its
bottom."

"There's something massive in there."
Plog pulled his boot back on. "And
Maynard seems to think he's a chicken."

"Does he?" Furp looked back into the

mist, his face frozen in horror. "Well, *that* really *is* a chicken!"

Plog's fur stood on end as a gigantic, ear-trampling squawk came out of the smog — soon followed by an equally gigantic but twice as terrifying chicken-monster. It was as big as a block of flats. Grey, metallic feathers bristled all over its body, with jagged edges that looked sharper than shark-teeth. Plog realized the twisted tree-trunk thing that had punted him out of the gas was one of the giant chicken's claws. Each leg was like a vast hillside of quivering muscle ending in tremendous talons that shook and split the ground wherever the monster stepped.

The bird-monster's face was perhaps its most fearsome feature. A beak as big as a truck curved out from beneath orange eyes shining like floodlights. A colossal red rubbery bit wobbled about on top of its head like an evil jelly.

But what scared Plog most of all was that he recognized the frightening figure. He'd seen its shadow enough times on two-way smellyvisions to know it anywhere – even two hundred times its usual size. "Furp," he breathed. "It . . . it's Lord Klukk!"

"It can't be!" said Furp weakly.

"Cluck!" said Maynard. "Cluck, cluck!"

"YES!" The chicken-beast's exultant squawk echoed around the Badlands. "I am Lord Klukk – facing you in the flesh at last."

"Can't say it's an improvement," Plog called bravely.

"*Buk-buk*-but it is!" Klukk boomed. "Now I can squash you like grapes *buk-buk*-beneath my feet!"

The spine-chilling chicken-monster raised one of his deadly claws, ready to bring it down on the Squaddies. Plog and Furp jumped aside as the foot thumped down and Maynard blundered into them. All three fell in a heap – then Maynard, still clucking, started to peck Plog in the face.

"Get off!" Plog cried. "We don't need chicken impersonators – we've got the real thing to deal with."

The king-sized Klukk turned with some difficulty and lifted a huge leg ready to attack again.

"You should split while you can, Maynard," Plog told him. "Your boss will crush you as well as us!" As the shadow of the fearsome foot fell over them, Danjo and Plog threw Maynard clear and barely dodged Klukk's claws themselves.

Marvin struggled up weakly. "Please, your lordliness," he cried. "Don't squash Maynard! He's accidentally breathed your special gas, and—"

"That idiot is of no further use to me," said Klukk. "And neither are *you* if you don't wake up your friends and get *buk-buk*-busy obeying my orders."

"What orders?" Plog demanded.

But then, with a roar of racing engines, the Slime-mobile came zooming up! Plog glimpsed Zill's determined face at the wheel – then the invisible monster truck smashed straight into Lord Klukk's gigantic legs. The feathery fiend staggered backwards, his red wobbly bits trembling with fury.

Danjo threw open the Slime-mobile's doors. "Plog, Furp, jump in!"

"We must bring Maynard with us," said Furp.

Plog frowned. "Bring that crazy guy? Why?"

"Because the smoke *made* him crazy," Furp explained, manhandling Maynard on board. "It must be some kind of . . . *chicken gas!*"

The super-enormous chicken-monster

was stamping back towards them, and Marvin and his two fellow hench-monsters were on their feet raising their chunky guns.

Plog threw himself into the Slime-mobile and Danjo slammed the door shut after him.

"Time we were gone," yelled Zill, stamping on the accelerator. Swinging the wheel hard left, she screeched away from Klukk and the encroaching smoke.

"Cluck, cluck," said Maynard, pecking at the floor as if searching for grain.

"Look at him," said Danjo. "In a world of his own."

"And if that smoke keeps spreading, it's a world we'll all be sharing." Plog pulled off his gas mask. "That crazy chicken-monster back there will turn *everyone* into crazy chicken-monsters. Trashland will be Klukk's for the taking!"

Chapter Four

WEAPONS OF MASS DIS-KLUKK-SHUN

Plog's words hung gloomily in the air as the Slime-mobile sped away from the giant gas cloud and the chilling chicken. But suddenly strange missiles started whizzing through the air. Explosions went off all around them, rocking the Slime-mobile. Wisps of gas curled out from the craters.

"It's Marvin and the maggots," Danjo realized. "They've got gas grenades!"

Furp nodded miserably. "As if that giant cloud of gas wasn't enough."

Plog checked the rear windscreen and saw it was true. The rotten maggots were firing their weird weapons high up into the air – and the grenades were raining down around the Squaddies, way too close for comfort.

"Zigzag, Zill," Plog shouted. "Make it harder for them to hit us."

"I'm on it," Zill assured him, swinging the truck from side to side. Slowly, the explosions faded as the Slime-mobile sped out of range.

"Well done, Zill," said Plog. "But it's round one to Klukk."

"I hate running away from him," said Zill.

Danjo shrugged. "What choice did we have? Next time we'll slime him – just wait."

"There's no time to wait," said Furp, pulling off his gas mask so he could get back to finishing Zill's and Danjo's. "Firing those gas grenades must be part of the plan Klukk mentioned."

"But why?" Plog cried. "There's a whole wall of gas at Klukk's back – why does he need grenades too?"

"I think I can answer that," said the All-Seeing PIE, his voice crackling out from the computer screen. "The Slime O'Clock News has just shown these pictures from the Dirty Nappy Dunes . . ."

39

Zill parked the Slime-mobile. "That's quite close by to here," she realized.

Plog and his friends watched the screen while Maynard pecked idly at the lav-lab's toilet. They saw maggot-men crawling over the huge squashy mounds of dirty nappies. Some were firing gas grenades down holes in the ground, others were shooting them high up into the air, clouding the stained peaks of the highest dunes with the eerie white mist.

"Of course!" Furp cried. "That gas cloud will sweep across Trashland but it won't reach the highest homes or underground burrows and sewers . . ."

Zill nodded. "So Klukk is using the maggots to get the gas into those hard-to-reach places."

"PIE," asked Plog, "what about the Nappy Dunes' population?"

"*Plop*-ulation, you mean," PIE corrected him. "So far, none of the natives have started acting like chickens. In fact, so far it seems the gas has had no effect."

Zill sniffed. "Ugh! What's that smell?"

Plog also caught a whiff – and choked.

"Danjo," he said accusingly. "Have you let one go?"

"Whoever said it was me, it was he," Danjo retorted.

Furp cleared his throat. "Sorry, everybody. It was me who produced the popping. I suspect it's a combination of  extreme fear and that roasted cockroach." He smiled sheepishly and held up two more futuristic faceplates. "Good job I've finished your gas masks, eh?"

"Cool." Danjo grabbed a mask as his own bot made a bubbling sound. "Oops!"

"Guys!" Zill groaned. "There's enough gas to deal with around here without you adding to it!"

Maynard took his head out of the toilet for a moment, a pained expression on his face. Then he stuck it back into the loo even harder than before.

Plog waved his tail like a fan

dispersing the niff. His tummy was gurgling too, but he held his own rude noises inside. "I just don't understand Lord Klukk," he said. "He's big and powerful and scary – so why has he stayed hidden up to now? How come he's always used other monsters to attack Trashland?"

"Maybe he's been working out," Danjo suggested.

"And if he's planning on turning everyone into brainless chicken-heads, why bother walking around in his own gas cloud?" Furp scratched his head. "It does seem quite peculiar. He's not even wearing a gas mask."

"Well, he's sort of a chicken anyway, isn't he?" Danjo argued. "A super-massive evil chicken. That must be why the gas doesn't affect him."

"I'll run some tests on Maynard," said Furp. "We must know more about this gas."

"In the meantime," Plog went on, "we'd better drive to the nearest towns in the Mucky Mattress Marshes and clear everyone away before the gas reaches them."

"They might be OK," said Danjo hopefully. "Like the Dunes-dwellers."

"Or they might go chicken-loopy," said Zill. "Like Maynard."

Plog sighed. "If we can't save Trashland, nobody can. The buck stops with us."

"*Buk!*" Maynard agreed.

Zill drove as fast as she could, but Plog still found the journey to the Mucky Mattress Marshes slow going. Furp had placed his techno-helmet on Maynard's head and was taking lots of mysterious measurements. Plog and Danjo just sat about feeling useless.

"*GROWWWL-BRRPP!*" went Plog's tum. "*Why* did I have that extra helping of roast cockroach?" he murmured miserably.

"Well, I've checked Maynard's brain activity," Furp reported. "And there isn't any! He really seems to have just a single thought in his head – that he's a chicken. Nothing else matters to him." He shook his head. "Once we've evacuated the mattress-mites, we can wait for the gas to roll in over the marshes and grab some in my jar for testing."

45

"I don't think you'll *have* to wait," Zill called grimly, slamming on the brakes. "Gas sighted – up ahead!"

"Oh, no . . ." Plog was first to join her at the front of the Slime-mobile, his heart sinking into his metal boots. A sprawling pile of bulky, battered mattresses loomed up ahead. Their faded patterns were all but lost beneath yukky stains, and rusted springs poked through like strange aerials. Sure enough, a thin white mist was already wafting about the damp landscape. The whistle and crump of falling gas grenades carried to the Squaddies' ears.

"The range on those maggots' guns must be further than we thought," Furp realized.

"Not that much further." Danjo pointed a pincer out through the rear windscreen. "Look!"

Plog, Furp and Zill turned to find a familiar wall of whirling whiteness was already visible on the horizon behind them.

"That gas cloud's picking up speed," said Zill helplessly.

Furp peered through a pair of binoculars. "And it looks like Lord Klukk's still just ahead of it."

Plog took the binoculars and nodded grimly as the sinister chicken-monster strode out from the fringes of the mist, maggot-men clinging to his feathers with one hand while firing grenades with the other. "He must have followed us," Plog breathed. "He knew we'd try to save the mattress-mites."

"Here come the mattress-mites now," said Zill.

Swinging back round to face front, Plog saw the mauve monsters come scuttling out of their soggy, under-stuffed mattress homes like the overblown bedbugs they resembled. Plog seemed to recall the mites were a quiet bunch who kept themselves to themselves. But he was sure their boggle eyes were not meant to look so black, and that their three antennae should look less droopy.

"They're not acting like chickens," Furp observed.

"No." Zill watched the mites mill about in the mist. "They look a bit . . . lost."

"ATTENTION!" A familiar squawk boomed out of the sky. "Calling all mattress-mites . . . Remember that you are the loyal servants of kindly Lord Klukk, ruler of all Trashland."

"What?" Plog spluttered.

"In another life," snorted Danjo.

But incredibly, uncannily, the mites began to nod their heads. "Yes!" the cry went up, spreading through the crowd. "Yes, we are. Of course we are."

"What are you on about?" Zill yelled through the windscreen.

49

"And remember, the Slime Squad are *buk-buk*-bad," Klukk declared, his voice louder and more terrible than ever. "Very, *very buk-buk*-bad. You hate them! They make you mad! They must *buk-buk*-be caught, crunched and cronkled."

"Cronkled?" Furp echoed blankly.

"YES!" roared the mites as one. "We hate the Slime Squad! They must be caught! They must be crushed!" The chorus of the crowd grew louder, angrier. "And at all costs, they must be cronkled!"

To Plog's disbelieving horror, the mattress-mites — eyes rolling with rage — began swarming towards the Slime-mobile, teeth bared . . .

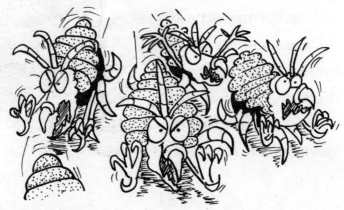

Chapter Five

"YOU ARE WHAT I SAY YOU ARE!"

Danjo gulped. "Those mattress-mites
don't seem to be acting like chickens."
He eyed the oncoming swarm. "In
fact, they look to be acting like highly-
trained catcher-cruncher-cronklers!"

"That's it!" Furp cried, making
everyone jump – even Maynard, who
plucked his head out of
the toilet in surprise.
"I know what the
gas does now –
and why Klukk
has to march
along with it."

51

"I don't think those marauding mites aim to give us a chance to chat about it," Zill growled, slamming the Slime-mobile into reverse. "How about you explain while I try to get us out of here?"

"It's not chicken gas!" Furp was hopping from seat to seat in his excitement. "It's a You-Are-What-I-Say-You-Are gas!"

Plog hung onto his own chair as Zill steered them bumpily backwards. "Huh? I don't get you."

"Remember when Maynard hared off into the gas without his protective helmet? You called him a chicken for running away . . ."

"So I did," Plog remembered. "I called him a chicken and he started to act like one."

"Exactly," said Furp. "And when these peaceful mattress-mites breathed in the gas, Klukk told them they were angry and that they wanted to get us."

"And sure enough, they *are* angry and they *do* want to get us!" said Danjo. "It's like they've been hypnotized!"

Plog ran to the lav-lab and grabbed Maynard. "You are *not* a chicken," he snapped. "You are Maynard the maggot-man. Do you hear me?"

"Cluck," said Maynard.

"It's no good." Furp tutted. "The hypno-gas makes its victims believe the first things they hear, and nothing more. That's why Klukk is out there in the smoke – giving his orders the moment his gas takes effect."

Danjo groaned. "And with a voice

that loud he can turn thousands of
monsters into his slaves in one go!"

"So why hasn't he told the monsters
in the Dirty Nappy Dunes what to do?"
Plog wondered.

No one had an answer – but Zill
certainly had a problem. "I can't drive
away fast enough in reverse," she yelled
over the straining roar of the engine.
The mattress-mites were still racing
towards them, clambering onto the
Slime-mobile's bonnet, whacking their
spindly arms against the windscreen,
battering the bodywork.

"Handbrake turn, Zill!" Plog shouted.

Zill yanked up hard on the handbrake while spinning the steering wheel hard left. The invisible truck screeched and skidded in a tight circle, shaking the mites free before juddering to a stop. But more of the bug-like monsters were already massing in the gas, pouring out of sticky holes in the Mucky Mattress marshland to catch, crunch and cronkle their supposed foes.

"That stunt was a hit – now it's time to split!" Danjo shouted.

Zill stamped on the accelerator and the chunky truck zoomed away from the smoky marshland. The marauding mites scuttled after them in a fury, but were soon lost from sight.

Plog wiped his furry brow. "That was too close."

"But what will we do when Klukk and his gas get to the next town?" asked Danjo. "We can't hope to outrun every monster in Trashland."

"And we didn't have a chance to get a sample of Klukk's gas," said Plog bitterly.

"Don't speak too soon," Furp told him as a familiar whistling, whooshing sound started up. *KRUMP!* A long-range gas shell burst open in the distance and white smoke curled up from inside it. "Klukk's started his bombardment again. He must be aiming for the Polystyrene Wilderness."

"ATTENTION, POLYSTYRENE PEOPLE," Klukk's distant voice boomed out. "You hate the Slime Squad . . . You will destroy them on sight . . ."

"I didn't think anything lived in that wilderness," said Danjo.

Furp nodded thoughtfully. "Clearly

he's taking no chances. No doubt he'll start bombarding Choketown next – and that *is* inhabited."

Danjo nodded. "Big, red burly monsters – you wouldn't want to get on the wrong side of *them*."

"Let's make for the Polystyrene Wilderness first," Plog decided. "It's on the way, and with any luck we can collect a gas sample there in peace."

But just then the engine spluttered and died and the Slime-mobile ground to a halt.

"We don't have any luck," said Zill crossly. "We're out of fuel. I don't understand it."

"There's a spare fuel can packed under the exhaust pipe," Danjo revealed, opening the doors and going outside. "Oh, *no!*"

"What is it?" Plog followed him outside, closely followed by Furp and Zill.

"When those mattress-mites attacked the Slime-mobile they put their teeth through our fuel tank," said Danjo. "All our fuel has leaked away."

"What about the spare can?" asked Zill hopefully.

"There's a hole in that too!" Danjo squirted slime-ice at the puncture to seal it. "There's only a little left – barely enough to get through the Polystyrene Wilderness to reach Choketown. We can't afford to waste any."

"And we can't afford to waste any more time either," said Plog. "We need

58

that gas sample, right away."

"Er . . . I think we might be about to get it too!" Furp pointed to the sky as a much louder whistling started up – and a massive explosion bloomed just to the right of them. "Klukk must've seen us stop – and he's trying to hit us!"

KA-KRUMMP! Another shell burst apart behind them and the shock wave threw Plog to the ground. He gasped to see a third shell sailing down from the clouds just overhead. "Klukk's bang on target this time," he yelled as the ominous whistle grew to an ear-piercing shriek. "And with the Slime-mobile stuck, we're sitting ducks!"

Chapter Six

POLYSTYRENE POWER

"Maybe not!" Zill jumped up and got busy with a new web of slime-strands, spitting them out sixteen to the dozen between the roof of the Slime-mobile and the ground. "Danjo, quick – fire as much thick, gooey slush under this lot as you can."

Plog watched her work. "What's the plan?"

"Soften the landing," she mumbled.

Furp got what she was driving at. "If the shell strikes something soft, it might not break open!"

The shell was almost on top of them, its high-pitched whistling drilling through their brains. Frantically Danjo sprayed a juicy pile of cold sludge under Zill's slime-net. With one end of the net fixed to the Slime-mobile, Furp and Plog took up the other end to make a kind of slushy hammock.

"Here it comes!" Danjo bellowed as the large metal ball finally fell with an almighty . . .

Ker-SQUELCH!

The gas grenade skimmed the side of

the Slime-mobile, hammered into the
net and splattered into the slush,
spattering the Squaddies with goo. Plog
held his breath . . .

But the shell did not go off.

"Yahooooo!" Zill jumped into the air.
"It worked!"

Plog gave Zill a big hug. "That was a
brilliant plan. Well done!"

"I can't wait to start studying this
stuff," said Furp. Then he held his tum as
it made a riotous gurgling sound. "But I
do wish that roast cockroach we all ate
would stop interrupting."

I wish I'd never touched it, thought Plog, holding his swollen tummy. Then he heard more whistling steal into the sky. "Come on, there'll be more shells dropping at any minute – and I don't fancy trying to catch them all!"

Danjo poured the last of their fuel into the tank and Zill slid back into the driver's seat. Furp moved Maynard the maggot-chicken away from the lav-lab and into Plog's seat so he could start his experiments. Plog watched the clever frog-monster as he drilled into the captured shell and drained off a little of the gas into his trusty toilet.

"Excellent," said PIE from the screen by the doors. "And not a moment too soon. The situation is growing worse.

My sensors show that gas attacks are taking place all over Trashland!"

"What?" Plog jerked in his seat. "Surely Klukk's voice can't be heard everywhere?"

"Klukk must have sent maggot squads with gas-grenade launchers far and wide," PIE said gravely. "And the maggots have been telling their unfortunate victims that they worship Lord Klukk and must battle anyone who says a word against him . . ."

The screen blurred to show trendy blue monsters in Goo York knocking down skyscrapers to build statues of Lord Klukk

in their place. It blurred again and showed junkjacks on Pongo Beach painting a huge chicken mural on the side of the Cast Iron Cliffs. Another change of scene showed brawling monsters in the Broken Furniture Valley – one bunch were waving wooden signs proclaiming Lord Klukk to be the best thing ever, and attacking anyone who dared to disagree.

"Why is he doing this?" cried Danjo.

PIE's face faded back into sight on the screen. "To cause chaos and confusion, thus splitting the population – so the rest of Trashland won't band together to stop him before his gas cloud engulfs everything."

Danjo's eyestalks drooped. "Even if we could clear all the monsters out of Choketown . . . where would we send them? Nowhere is safe!"

"This could be the end of the world," murmured Plog, and his bottom rumbled as if in pained agreement. "And with our fuel almost out, it looks like Choketown will be the scene of our final stand."

"Cheer up," said PIE brightly. "The Dirty Nappy Dunes are full of gas, but still the Dunes-dwellers seem unaffected – well, apart from bumping into each other a lot because they can't see where they're going. And there are no reported cases in the Poo-nited States either . . ."

"Yet," muttered Zill.

"Hey!" Danjo said suddenly, tapping his head. "An idea is here!"

Plog was glad for a distraction. "Oh?"

"What if we could make more gas masks?" Danjo jumped up. "We wouldn't

have to evacuate anybody – they could just wear the masks and stay safe until we beat the gas."

Plog grinned. "Fantastic plan!"

"I'll give you my designs," said Furp, "then you can get to work."

Danjo nodded. "How many monsters are there in Choketown?"

"About five thousand," Furp replied, fiddling with his instruments.

"And how many extra gas masks can we make?" Danjo asked eagerly.

"Er . . ." Furp considered. "Two."

Plog's ears drooped. "Two?"

"Only four thousand, nine hundred and ninety-eight more monsters to worry about then," Danjo sighed as Furp passed him some papers. "Still, I guess every little helps . . ."

Within the hour, the Squaddies had reached the barren, pitted plains of the Polystyrene Wilderness – and come up against a huge white cube of packaging lying across the track.

"A polystyrene roadblock," Zill noted, slipping on her gas mask. "We need to shift it."

Plog shivered as he put on his own gas mask and stepped outside. The white expanses of the Wilderness were made whiter still by the creeping gas filling every crack and crevice.

Zill scampered down, and she and Plog crossed to the polystyrene blocking their path. Plog dug his fingers into the cube and heaved – accidentally pulling off a huge white chunk as he did so.

"Ow!" came a dry, throaty gargle.

Zill jumped. "What was that?"

But Plog couldn't answer. He was speechless with shock as a huge, craggy figure detached itself from the cube – a thing of living polystyrene!

"You just broke off one of my feet," rasped the boxy thing, two vivid pink eyes blinking open in his jagged head.

"Um, sorry," said Plog.

"Hang on." The burning pink eyes narrowed. "You're part of the Slime Squad, aren't you?"

"Er . . . no!" Zill said quickly. "Never

heard of them."

"You are! You are my enemies!" With a scraping, scrunching noise the polystyrene person got to his five remaining feet and raised fists like huge white bricks. "I must destroy you!"

"*We* must destroy you," came a sinister chorus from all around. To Plog and Zill's horror, more of the mysterious monsters came crunching to life, rising up from the layers of polystyrene all around, pink eyes shining with hate and heavy hands set to crush the Squaddies flat . . .

"Here we go again!" Plog stared up at the polystyrene warriors. "We're not your enemies! There's this gas, see. It's allowed a giant mutant chicken to hypnotize you—"

"Destroy!" roared the nearest towering monster. The hard white slab of his fist slammed down towards him . .

Zill pushed Plog clear and the polystyrene punch just barely missed. "I don't think they're listening, Fur-boy. And we haven't got time to waste convincing them. Look!"

Plog glanced behind – and saw a huge army of mattress-mites swarming over the top of a wide polystyrene hillside.

The hillside too was coming to life as scores of many-legged monsters cracked apart from the piles of packaging.

"We've got to get out of here!" Zill cried.

Plog shoved hard at the legs of the white monster towering over them, who fell in a tumble. "That's the roadblock cleared. But we'll never outrun the reinforcements!"

Zill gulped to see a tidal wave of mattress-mites and mighty white monsters approaching fast down the hillside towards them . . .

Chapter Seven

NIT!

"One chance!" Zill lashed out a slime-
line and lassoed a big chunk of
polystyrene at the base of the mound.
"Give me a hand, Fur-boy."

Plog joined her in tugging on the
big brick, his muscles straining to
their limit – and as the piece
finally pulled clear, the entire
hill above it began to
collapse. Shouting in
dismay, the hypnotized
monsters fell with it,
crashing down with
a squeaky, dusty
bang.

"Right," said Plog. "Run!"

"You cannot escape me for ever, Slimy Simpletons!" Now the hill had been levelled, the giant Lord Klukk was visible once again before his towering curtain of smoke. His voice echoed out at a billion decibels. "Soon I shall have total control over Trashland."

"So why is he so bothered about stopping us now?" Plog panted as they bundled back on board the Slime-mobile.

Zill pushed Maynard out of the way and hopped into the driver's seat. "It can only mean there *is* a way to stop his gruesome gas – and he's worried that we will find it!"

"I reckon you're right." Plog turned to Furp, still hard at work in the lav-lab beside Danjo. "Any progress?"

PIE's computerized face appeared on the screen. "Do not disturb Furp now. I believe he is very close to a breakthrough."

"I'm very close to a break-*wind*," Plog muttered as his tum chugged and bubbled again. "Danjo, how are you getting on?"

The crab-creature held up a single mask. "What's the panic?"

"The mattress-mites have been joined by some pink-eyed polystyrene," Plog explained. "Klukk's got the population of two whole towns after us. You've got to find a cure, Furp – you've just got to!"

"I'm trying!" Furp assured him.

The tense journey continued in silence – save for the gurgle of tender tummies and the bubble of concoctions in Furp's strange tests. Plog helped Danjo finish gas mask number two. Maynard clucked.

Zill drove them over rickety bridges and treacherous swamps. But as they neared Choketown, her heart plummeted into her roach-stuffed tum. "We're too late," she gasped. "Klukk's smoke – it's everywhere!"

Plog jumped up, nudged Maynard aside and joined her at the front. Sure enough, the lights of Choketown were shining dimly through a dark purple haze, like a big bruise on the landscape.

"It's OK," Danjo assured them. "Choketown's always smoky and smoggy and dusty – that's how it got its name. There are so many factories, mines and refineries there that the air is really filthy."

Zill turned up her nose. "How does anyone manage to live here?"

"Well, every hour the fans come on," Danjo explained. "Look, it's happening now!"

The dark clouds over Choketown were starting to curl and whirl. Suddenly they began to streak slowly away in all directions, thinning out. At first, all Plog could see was a tall tower, its square roof crowned with an impressive array of massive electric fans, whirring and whooshing the air pollution away. Slowly the rest of Choketown came into sight – an ugly collection of coal pits and furnaces,

smelting works and smoking chimneys,
all stained black with dirt. Even as the
fans died down, the dirty clouds began
to gather again and hide the town
from view.

"Not the prettiest place in the world,"
Zill remarked as she started to drive
closer.

"And the monsters who work there
are as hard as atomic nails," Danjo
reminded them.

Suddenly Furp leaped
in the air. "Perhaps we
won't have to worry
about them turning
against us!" he cried.
"I might have found
the answer!"

Plog's ears shot straight
up and Danjo's eyes bulged to the size
of beach balls.

"Well, what is it?" Zill asked excitedly,
wagging her tail.

"The cure's been within our power all along, I'm sure of it," Furp twittered. "Right under our poor little noses. Now, I *must* test it out on Maynard here. Get ready to open the windows! Er, Maynard?"

But Maynard clucked sulkily and shook his head. "*Buk-buk!*"

"Don't be in a grump just because I pulled your head out of the toilet," Furp told him. "We don't have time to waste."

"Cluck, cluck, CLUCK!" said Maynard rudely, and suddenly started running about the Slime-mobile like a headless chicken-maggot, flapping his arms and squawking like a looper. CRUNCH! He crashed into the lav–lab's workbench and sent the experiments flying. Test tubes broke open and beakers split.

Bubbling goo splashed over Furp's crash helmet and set it on fire! The image of PIE on the smellyvision set vanished into static.

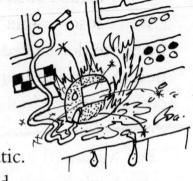

"No!" Furp wailed, leaping to the rescue of his headpiece, blowing as sparks spat and spurted from inside. "Oh, dear!"

Maynard started pecking at the workbench beside him as though it were covered in tasty grain, cracking open a jar as he did so.

"Look at what you've done," Danjo yelled crossly. "You crazy nit!" He quickly fired slime at the helmet, putting out the flames, while Plog grabbed Maynard and sat him on the toilet before he could do any more damage.

"Furp," Zill called urgently. "Is the crash helmet badly broken?"

Plog flicked switches on the screen. "We've lost contact with PIE. But I guess we don't need him right now if you've found the cure for the hypnogas, right?" He looked at Furp, who was staring down at the helmet. "Er . . . Furp?"

Furp made no reply. And then Plog saw a tiny wisp of white smoke escape the broken jar on the desk. "Gas masks, quickly!" he roared.

Danjo and Zill quickly followed Plog's example and put on their masks. But Furp just went on staring – and then he jumped through the air and landed on Plog's back, pulling on his fur.

"Hey!" Plog cried. "Furp, what are you doing?"

"I'm a nit!" Furp squeaked. "A crazy nit!" He rolled his eyes and crawled over Plog's back. "Ohhh, look what I've done. Nit, nit, NIT!"

"Oh no!" Zill wailed. "Furp must have breathed in the gas!"

Danjo slapped a pincer to his forehead. "And when I told Maynard that he was a nit and to look at what he'd done, Furp heard it as a hypnotic command."

Plog managed to pull Furp off from his back. "The cure, Furp! Do you remember the cure?"

"Cure?" Furp frowned as if struggling to remember, then stared at the workbench. "Yes, look at what I've done – I've found a cure!"

"Please, Furp, what is it?" Zill begged him.

"It's . . . nnnnnnnnnnnnnn- *nit* possible to say!" Furp laughed, hopping about crazily. "Nit, nit, nit."

"*Buk-buk-buk*," said Maynard, apparently approving of this change in his captor.

"It's no good." Plog covered his eyes. "We've lost Furp, we've lost contact with PIE, *and* we've lost our last chance of finding a cure for the gas in time."

"Look!" Furp said, pointing to the floor. "Look at what I've done!"

Zill frowned. "He hasn't done something gross, has he?"

"No." Plog saw that Furp was pointing to some pieces of paper on the floor, and stooped to pick them up. "Hmm . . . it looks like Furp was making notes."

"Nits!" Furp chirruped, hopping onto Danjo's crimson shoulder.

"No, *notes*," Danjo told him.

"Look at what I've done!" Furp said again. "Look! Look!"

"These are notes on the cure!" Plog beamed. "Even hypnotized, Furp's trying to help us."

"Nit!" Furp stuck out his tongue and shook his head.

"Wubble-wubble-wubble."

"Or possibly not," Plog admitted. Then he gasped. "He's written down here, 'Strong wind could be the answer'."

"Strong wind?" Danjo smiled slowly. "Hey, that makes sense. A strong wind would blow all the gas away! Right?"

"Right," called Zill. "All the way back to the Badlands where it can't hurt anyone else."

Plog nodded. "And maybe a sudden gale in the face will jolt the gassed-up monsters back to their senses."

"But it's not windy today," Zill pointed out. "So how does that help?"

Danjo and Plog had the same thought at exactly the same time. "The fans of Choketown!" they cried together.

Zill turned a somersault in her seat. "Yes! Brilliant!"

"Step on it, Zill," Plog told her. "Once we're going really fast we can stick Furp's head out of the window so he gets the breeze."

"He *said* we should open the windows," Danjo recalled. "It all makes sense!"

But as Zill increased speed, the engine began to splutter. "Oh no," she said.

"We're finally running out of fuel – and we've barely reached the outskirts of Choketown."

"Double 'oh no'!" Plog cringed as a familiar whistle-and-crump went off somewhere close by. Wisps of gas blew up around them as with a last rasp and splutter the Slime-mobile conked out completely. "We're trapped here, and Klukk's long-range gas grenades are landing again – ready to turn every tough guy in town against us!"

Chapter Eight
FAN-TASTIC

"Come on," said Plog, putting on his gas mask and picking up the spares. "Those fans on the central tower are our last chance – we'll just have to reach them on foot."

"Nit," Furp agreed, and Maynard pecked him.

"We'd better take Furp with us," Plog added. "The mattress-mites and polystyrene people are still out to get us all, and they'll be here soon."

"We must take Maynard too," said Zill. "He's a creep but we can't just abandon him."

"ATTENTION CHOKETOWN!" The ground-shaking squawk of the colossal Klukk carried over the roar of exploding shells. "THE SLIME SQUAD ARE YOUR ENEMIES – DESTROY THEM!"

Zill stamped her feet crossly as she put on her mask. "It's just nonstop danger out there!"

"True." Plog winked at her. "And that's where we're going. Because when danger looms large ..."

Danjo and Zill joined in with the war cry: "The Slime Squad shout 'CHARRRRRRGE!'"

And the three Squaddies charged outside with the stricken Furp and Maynard – into the war zone that Choketown had become. The blast of explosions split the smoking air, and a familiar white gas was seeping into sight. Many of Choketown's burly red workers ran about in alarm, but some were turning glassy-eyed as the gas got to them.

"DESTROY THE SLIME SQUAD!" Klukk repeated at top volume.

"Time we weren't here." Danjo raised his right pincer and sprayed a flat strip of slime-ice over the ground ahead of them, like a pathway. "We don't want to be late – so let's skate!"

He set off on his three sturdy peg-legs, and Plog and Zill skidded after him, making for Choketown's central tower, the metal fans at its top shining in the moonlight like a beacon of hope. Faster and faster they skated, leaping over lunging workers, dodging gas grenades, ignoring Furp's *nits* and Maynard's *clucks*, focusing only on the tower. And as they finally approached it, Plog saw four grim-faced night watchmen in

smart uniforms outside the main doors.

"Hey!" wheezed the biggest one in a voice like a sickly engine. "Isn't that the Slime Squad?"

"Dang well looks like it!" His smaller friend had a much louder voice. "They'll sort out this mess, you'll see."

"Result!" cheered Danjo. "The gas hasn't reached here yet!"

Ker-KRUMP! White mist rose up around the night watchmen's feet.

"You spoke too soon," Plog groaned.

"No way am I standing for this," Zill shouted, "and neither are they!" She spat out two slime-lines and lassoed the monsters who'd called out. With a giant jerk of her head she tugged them clear of the gas and onto the slimy ice path Danjo had provided. Suddenly the startled night watchmen found themselves lying on the slippery ground at Plog's feet!

Plog plonked down Furp and pulled the Slime Squad's two spare gas masks onto the guards' faces. "Quickly," he said. "Who are you?"

"I'm Bolli," rasped the biggest one.

"And dang me if I'm not Frit," his friend said loudly.

"Nit!" said Furp.

"No, *Frit.*"

Bolli scratched his rough, bald head. "What in Trashland is going on around here?"

"No time to explain right now," Zill said breathlessly, "but we need to get to the fans on your central block."

"It's our job to protect the fans, Miss Zill," said Frit. "If anything happened to them Choketown would be lost in smoke for ever."

Plog felt his stomach bubble and tighten as more gas shells fell all around them. "All of Trashland will be lost in smoke for ever if we don't get up to those fans fast!"

"Oi! Slime Squad! No!" bawled two other guards from the cloud of gas, rushing forward to attack. "You're our worst enemies. We'll get you . . ."

Frit's red face filled with a frown. "What the heck's up with them?"

"The gas isn't good." Plog flattened  one guard with his toughest punch and Danjo decked the other with a crunch of his claw. "That's why we need to blow it away and bring everyone back to their senses."

"We're with you," said Bolli. "The fan controls are up on the roof with the fans. Follow us!"

He and Frit led the way to the heavy main doors and opened them with a big key. Once Plog, Zill and Danjo had dragged Furp and Maynard inside, Frit locked the doors again behind them.

Bolli raced up a large spiral staircase built around a huge generator that powered the phenomenal fans. The air felt charged with energy, and Plog's fur prickled as he followed Bolli higher and higher into the building.

At last they burst out into the middle of a large square the size of a boxing ring. The fans that ringed the tower's edges stood still and silent for now. White gas drifted about with the usual smoke and smog.

As he looked down over Choketown, Plog felt sick. His head throbbed, his stomach ached and his bottom felt ready to explode. But he held his gas in for Zill and Danjo's sake.

95

Things were bad enough already. Scores of the town's red-skinned residents were marching on the central block, pouring out from the mines and factories. Behind them swarmed hundreds of mattress-mites and polystyrene people – all hypnotized into thinking that Plog and his friends were public enemies that had to be destroyed. And behind *them*, the massive, misshapen monster that was Lord Klukk was marching tirelessly out of the white smoke, cackling with glee.

Frit gulped. "I never saw nothing like this before, Bolli."

Bolli was wide-eyed. "Me neither, Frit."

"Switch on the fans," Plog yelled at them. "Strong wind will put things right."

"I dang well hope that *something* can."
Frit crossed to a large control panel built
into the ground. He and Bolli turned
wheels and pulled down on levers, and
slowly the fans began to turn.

Holding his own grumbly tum, Danjo
studied the controls. "Frit, Bolli – put the
power to maximum."

The guards nodded. Soon the thrum
of the mega-strong fans was like the
breath of giants, growing louder and
louder. A huge gale was quickly blasting
across Choketown. The smoke began
to whirl away.

Dirt and dust and grit whipped through the air. The wind blew so hard that the fires in the town's furnaces began to blow out!

Plog crossed to the edge of the roof between two of the fans, staring out at the murderous monsters gathered below as they weathered the sudden storm.

"They're feeling a strong wind now," Danjo declared.

But then a shout went up. "There's the furry Squaddie – Blog, or whatever his name is."

"And Danjo too," another monster shouted. "Get them! Find the others and get them all!"

The mob pushed forward, smashing at the doors as the call was taken up – "Get them all!"

"Cluck," chuckled Maynard.

"Nit," said Furp sadly.

"It . . . it hasn't worked!" Plog turned to face his friends as Klukk's evil laughter rang out over the chanting mob. "Furp was wrong about the wind. We just lost our last hope. Nothing can save Trashland now!"

Chapter Nine

THE WIND OF CHANGE

As Plog stared out over the sea of raging monsters and the mad chicken-beast who controlled them, his delicate tum could take no more. His butt let rip with a roaring raspberry that left even burly Bolli looking queasy.

"That's not helping, Fur-boy!" Zill choked, her eyes watering. "I can smell it through my gas mask. What a niff!"

"Sorry," said Plog, blushing. "Quick, let's angle the fans *down*wards and try to blow those crowds away from the tower doors."

Danjo and Zill started pointing the nearest propellers at the milling monsters. But then Danjo parped too. "Whoops! Pardon."

Frit clutched his throat. "What the heck have you been eating?"

"Roast Cockroach *à la* Slime with all the trimmings," said Furp. "I cooked it myself."

"Yeah," said Danjo. "And it's given us all the worst gas we ever ..." He blinked and did a double take. "Furp?"

"Furp, you spoke like you're normal!" Zill beamed.

"Then . . ."
Plog grabbed
the frog-
monster by the
shoulders.
"You're not a
nit any more?"

"Correct!"
Furp grinned. "And
it's all thanks to your
bottoms!"

Zill groaned. "He's not better at all.
He might not be nitty, but he's definitely
nutty!"

"No, I'm not," Furp insisted. "I assure
you that Plog's bottom *did* put me
right." He smiled at Frit and Bolli and
looked around at the fans, taking in the
situation in seconds. "So, you found my
notes, hmm? But I fear you
misunderstood them."

"Did we?" Plog was puzzled. "Strong
wind could be the answer, you said."

"Yes," said Furp impatiently. "I meant strong *bottomly* wind – such as the gas we've got after eating my slimy roast!" He bounced about in excitement. "Get on with tilting the fans towards those monsters down below. Quickly!"

With new enthusiasm, Plog, Zill and Danjo set to work, heaving at the fans' heavy mounts. Frit and Bolli lent their strength as Furp went on explaining.

"I was trying to work it out," he began, shouting to be heard over the whoosh of the fans and the yelling and banging of the masses below. "Why the Dirty Nappy Dunes and the Poo-nited States should stay unaffected when Klukk's gas was working fine everywhere else. And then it hit me . . ."

Zill gasped. "Because those are the stinkiest places in Trashland?"

"Precisely," Furp agreed. "A strong stink stops the spell." He pointed at Maynard, who was pecking about on the roof edge, watching the fans as they spun. "When I broke wind back in the Slime-mobile, I thought Maynard seemed affected for a moment. But then he put his head back down the lav-lab's loo where the air was fresher, and the moment – like the fart – was lost."

The pounding on the tower doors had grown deafening – soon the rabble would break in. Teeth gritted, Plog and Frit aimed the final fan towards ground level. "So what we need to do . . ." Plog grunted, "is send a bad smell blowing through all of Trashland."

"That's right," Furp agreed. "So stick your behinds in front of those fans and GET THOSE BOTTOMS BLAZING!"

Danjo grinned. "My rear's in gear –
I've been holding bad smells in for
ages!" He pushed his bottom towards
the fan and a loud raspberry blew
above the din. The foul smell was
whipped away by the super-spinning
fan blades and went straight to work. A
dozen monsters passed out at once!
Many more began to look a bit wobbly
on their feet. Within moments the
banging on the
door grew less
insistent.

"What are we doing?" one said.

"Who did we want to get again?"

Zill clapped her paws. "It's working!" She rushed over to the other side of the roof and squeezed between the fans. "Let me have a go . . ." Zill's bottom out-performed Danjo's in volume *and* smelliness – and no sooner had she popped than the fan's gale propelled it into the mob far below.

"Hey!" A muscle-bound Choketowner frowned. "What gives?"

"Where's my nice damp mattress?" asked a muddled mite. "What am I doing here?"

"How should I know?" said the polystyrene person beside him. "I'm just a talking lump of packaging!"

106

Furp hopped right on top of a fan, adjusted his round metal pants and let rip. "Keep going," he urged his friends.

Bolli barged up to him. "I'm not a superhero, but would an ordinary fart help?"

"The smellier it gets around here, the better," Furp assured him.

Bolli bared his bot and got busy too, while Frit yelled encouragement. "Get those cheeks bursting, everybody!"

"Toot away to save the day!" Danjo agreed. But then he gulped and pointed to the sinister form of Lord Klukk striding through the town. "With that whopping great chicken on the way, it won't be hard!"

Plog raised his tail and set his furry behind against a fan on the fourth side of the building. But after hours of trying to hold his bad air in, he found now that he couldn't let out a single pop! "Come on, butt," he muttered, straining away. "Don't clam up on me now!" He looked at Furp. "Shall I take off my boots and stink them out with my slimy feet?"

"I'm afraid the smell needs to be a really toilety one," Furp told him. "On this occasion, your rotten feet can't help us!"

Luckily the efforts of the others were winning the day alone. The more Danjo, Zill and Furp bombarded the horde below with bottom blasts, the

more the gas was overwhelmed. Klukk's hypnotic hold on his victims was weakening. The shouts of "Destroy!" were being drowned out by shouts of "Why aren't I in bed?" and "Isn't that the Slime Squad?" and "Ooooh! A living piece of polystyrene!"

"*Noooo!*" Lord Klukk's pained, chickenish squawk broke across the sky like thunder as the mountain-sized monster bore down on Choketown. "I won't *buk-buk*-be *buk-buk*-beaten again! You may know the secret of defeating my hypno-gas *buk-buk*-but you will not live to tell of it!"

"Clear the area, everyone!" Frit bellowed. "Giant killer chicken coming through!"

Zill spat out slime-lines and used them as extra-long whips to help scatter the crowds. Danjo did the same with squirts of chilly slime. At the same time, Furp and Bolli helped Plog angle the fans upward again, pointing them towards Klukk and the huge wall of encroaching white smoke at his back.

"No! Stop that!" spluttered the chicken-beast, his hefty feathers rattling in the fierce wind. The gas cloud was torn apart and soon gusted away. The maggot-men clinging onto Klukk's bloated body tried firing their gas grenades, then wailed helplessly as they were blown clear away, crash-landing amongst the fleeing monsters.

"Those maggot critters helped mess with your minds!" Frit bawled at the crowds. "Run them out of town!"

Since the monsters in the square were already running from the gigantic looming chicken, it was little effort for them to chase the maggots away as they did so.

"Curse you, Squaddies!" His beak set in an evil grimace, Klukk forced his way towards the tower as the tornado raged around him. "I shall wreck your fans and then crush you without mercy!"

"He's getting closer," Zill groaned.

"Perhaps we can boost the fans' power?" Plog suggested, his tum still gurgling.

But even as he spoke, the racing whoosh of the fans cut suddenly dead. The wind dropped in an instant.

Frit swapped a terrified look with Bolli. "The dang power's cut off!"

"He did it!" Bolli pointed a fat red finger – at Maynard. "Him!"

"Of course!" Furp clutched his head. "Maynard smelled our blow-offs and turned back to normal too!"

"I turned off the fans, my lord!" the maggot-man yelled, climbing onto the edge of the roof. "Now you can get the Squaddies!"

Frit punched Maynard to the ground – but Klukk was already charging forwards through the now-empty courtyard, vast wings flapping. And a second later, his breathtaking beak had

112

swung closed with a cringe-making
crunch – around Plog!

Chapter Ten
GLORIOUS DEFEAT

Zill screamed and Danjo fired hot and cold slime at Klukk, but the mega-chunky chicken-monster only laughed through a beakful of prime Plog.

"Guys, get out of here!" Plog gasped and groaned as Klukk's beak pressed down on his tender tummy. "Run! I'll hold him off." He struggled and kicked with all his strength at the inside of the massive yellow mouth,

but it was like striking solid steel
– CLANG! CLANG! *CRACK!*

Eh? Plog thought. *Sounds like glass breaking.*

"You furry flophead!" Klukk's voice rang out all around him, dire and deafening. "Your oversized *buk-buk*-boots cracked my window! I shall squash you for that!"

Plog frowned. *Why would he have a window inside his beak?*

"Hey! Klukk's voice isn't muffled," Furp realized. "Even though he's chomping down on Plog!"

Plog moaned in agony. Earlier, he'd had no luck trying to fire up his bot – but with this monumental beak crushing his stomach, the pressure was building and building inside his gurgling, grumbling body until –

FRRRRFRRRR-PLPLPLPLPLPLPLLLL!

With a noise like the biggest balloon in the universe deflating, Plog's bottom banks burst at last. The phenomenal fart exploded like a ton of dynamite right inside Klukk's beak! The glass Plog had already cracked now shattered in the bum-blast. The smell was enough to make a cast-iron orang-utan with no nose self-destruct in a moment . . .

And just enough to make a giant chicken-shaped monster collapse!

"Too toxic . . . *buk-buk*-blacking out . . ." As Klukk keeled over, his head smashed down on top of the central tower, crushing a line of fans as he fell.

"Plog!" yelled Zill. She, Furp and Danjo rushed forward to rescue their leader from the evil lord's beak. Danjo forced his pincers inside and strained to separate the giant jaws until – ker-KLUNK! – the bottom of the beak broke off with a clatter and Plog rolled clear.

"This beak is solid brass!" Furp boggled. "The feathers are made of metal and rubber. Klukk's giant body is only a costume. He's a phony!"

"But what about Plog?" Zill asked anxiously. "Are you all right, Fur-boy?"

"I think so." Plog patted his tum. "My indigestion has gone anyway. Better out than in, I guess!"

"And we'd better drag out whoever's been hiding inside this oversized chicken suit," growled Danjo.

"That gas explosion of yours broke open the suit's control centre," said Furp, peering at a shattered glass window at the back of the beak. "Whoever's inside must've looked out from here."

"Let's see," said Zill. She spat a slime-line into the broken beak's depths and then yanked it out. Tangled in the end of the sticky rope was a tiny, scrawny figure with fluffy white feathers, little black eyes and a delicate beak.

Plog stared. "Who are you?"

"I . . . am Lord Klukk," chirped the little creature.

Maynard sat up groggily. "YOU?" He looked horrified. "But . . . you're cute and sweet!"

"How dare you!" snarled Klukk, trying to act all mean — but somehow he just seemed even cuter. "I am your evil master! I am destined to rule!"

"Come off it. You're just a lovely little chick." Maynard shuddered. "No wonder you always spoke to us through smellyvision sets, with lights set up to make your shadow look yukky and scary." He jumped up and ran away. "Well, I'm off. Me and my maggot-mates will be laughing stocks if it ever gets out that we served a tiny chicken. We'll never work for you again!"

"Come *buk-buk*-back!" Klukk yelled. "This is just a minor problem. I can still triumph over all monsters!"

"Don't think so," said Plog. "You're so tiny you couldn't even duff up a dust-mite. You don't even *look* like a monster."

"I'm not. I'm *buk-buk*-better," Klukk bragged. "My grandmother was the pet hen of Godfrey Gunk himself – creator of Trashland!"

Zill's eyes widened. "You know about Godfrey Gunk, the mad genius inventor?"

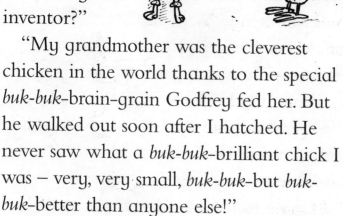

"My grandmother was the cleverest chicken in the world thanks to the special *buk-buk*-brain-grain Godfrey fed her. But he walked out soon after I hatched. He never saw what a *buk-buk*-brilliant chick I was – very, very small, *buk-buk*-but *buk-buk*-better than anyone else!"

Danjo snorted. But Plog shushed him, fascinated.

121

"My family laughed at me when I said I was an evil genius. So I left Godfrey's garden for the wild wilderness of the rubbish dump *buk-buk-*beyond." Klukk glared at Bolli and Frit. "Little things like you were all over the place. I had to rule you! I employed evil monsters to help me and even learned how to create my own toxic creatures . . ."

Furp tutted. "But why?"

"I had to take over the world to prove to my *buk-buk*-brothers and sisters that I was the *buk-buk*-best!" claimed Klukk. "And when my hypno-gas reaches Godfrey Gunk's garden I'll control them as well as everyone else. Finally they will see what a diabolical mastermind I am!"

"So," Plog breathed. "*That's* why you wanted to take over Trashland."

Danjo nodded. "Just to show off!"

Furp looked at Zill. "We live in Godfrey Gunk's house, and I've never seen any chickens there."

"Me neither," Zill agreed. "They must all have moved away, ages ago."

"So all his scheming has been for nothing," Plog concluded. "I know he's crazy and evil and all that . . . but I actually feel a bit sorry for him."

"I know what you mean," said Furp.

"But what can we do with him?" Danjo wondered. "He'll always be up to bad stuff."

"Hey!" Frit called from the edge of the tower. "Now this big chicken suit's fallen over we can see where the gas is coming from."

Bolli nodded. "From its oversized butt!"

"Of course!" Plog ran over to see thick white smoke drifting from the enormous chicken's tail feathers. "That's why Klukk was always walking near the front of his smog cloud – he was pushing it out as he went along."

"And that's why he needed such a big suit," Furp realized. "It must be a walking hypno-gas factory!"

124

"Good job we're still wearing our gas masks," said Zill.

"But Klukk doesn't have one," Plog murmured. "And that gives me an idea ..." He crouched and got closer to Klukk as the smoke began to wisp around them. "Now, listen to me, Klukk. You are a very happy, lovely little chicken."

"*What?*" screeched Klukk. But then the gas got up his beak and he smiled a little sleepily. "Um ... happy and lovely, you say?"

"Very happy and extremely lovely," Plog assured him. "And you are never happier than when you are pecking about all by yourself – as far from the

125

Darkest Corner and the Murky Badlands as you can get." He smiled at his friends. "In fact, somewhere in the empty wild lands beyond the Car Wreck Coast would be good . . ."

"I'll go at once!" Klukk declared with a big grin. "I'm so happy! Isn't it *buk-buk*-brilliant? I *love* pecking about by myself . . ." He flapped on top of the head of his massive chicken suit and slid all the way down its back to the square below. "WHEEEEEE!"

"It's over," Furp whispered, watching Klukk skip merrily away into the distance.

"We beat him!" Danjo grabbed Plog

in a huge, crusty hug. "You used Klukk's own weapon against him!"

"Fantastic plan, Fur-boy," Zill agreed.

"But that gas is still spurting out from the big chicken's bum," Frit fretted.

"Not for long!" Furp hopped into the shattered control room at the back of the brass beak and started fiddling with wires and switches. "Whatever blows out can be made to suck up . . . like so!"

As Plog and his friends watched, the gas began vanishing inside the huge, feathery backside as if a giant hoover was hidden within! The chicken suit began to fill up like a vast inflatable. Finally it rose into the air and started to drift away.

"There!" Furp grinned. "It should float back to the Badlands, sucking in gas as it goes. If my calculations are right, it should eventually pop harmlessly high over the Darkest Corner!"

"Wa-hooooo!" Danjo punched the air. "Furp LeBurp, you're a genius!"

"But what about the rest of the gas drifting over Trashland?" asked Zill.

"We'll just have to spread nasty smells all over the land," said Plog. "That will soon break the hypnotic hold."

"Ooooh, can we help?" asked Bolli. "We've always wanted to go on a tour of Trashland, haven't we, Frit?"

Frit nodded keenly. "And our bottoms are well up for the challenge." He tooted so hard that a nearby fan fell over. "See?"

"That smells horrible!" Danjo gasped for breath. "They've got the job as far as I'm concerned!"

"Thanks." Bolli let off with happiness, and ran away with Frit. "You four are the greatest!"

"You know what?" said Danjo, grinning round at his fellow Squaddies as they stared out over Trashland. "I think he might just be right!"

Back at the Slime Squad's secret base, the All-Seeing PIE was watching Lord Klukk vanish happily into the distance.

"That's one menace defeated," he murmured. "But there are many other evil monsters lurking in the Badlands. And now Klukk has gone, the worst of the worst will be battling it out to take his place as Trashland's Most Wanted. The Slime Squad will be needed to protect the innocent more than ever . . ." PIE chuckled. "Which will suit them down to the ground!"

He tuned his electronic sensors to the top of Choketown's tower and proudly watched his team celebrate their victory. The future might be full of menace, but the present was a time for fun.

And as he joined Furp, Zill and Danjo in a vigorous rooftop conga, Plog couldn't remember ever feeling happier.

"It's been an amazing six months for the Slime Squad," Furp declared. "And the newspooper reports of our victory today will finish off Plog's special scrapbook a treat!"

"Now we can *really* party when we get back to base," said Zill.

"You can count on me for some wild dancing," said Danjo. "But I bet the months ahead will be even wilder!"

Plog looked up at the moon and the stars in the crystal-clear skies and sighed dreamily. "I wonder what other slimy adventures lie in store for us?"

"Lots, Fur-boy." Zill kissed him on the cheek and spun him round and round in a dance of pure happiness, as the moon shone smiling down. "Lots and lots and lots and *lots*!"

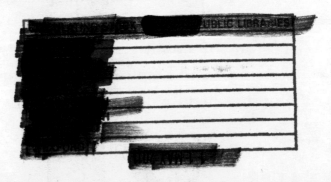